I. I. STEVENS SCHOOL
1242 - 18th East
Seattle, Washington 98102

The Way
to Windra

The Way to Windra

BY

Patricia Goehner Baehr

ILLUSTRATED BY GAIL OWENS

FREDERICK WARNE
New York   London

Copyright © 1980 by Patricia Goehner Baehr
Frederick Warne & Co., Inc.
New York, New York
Library of Congress Cataloging in Publication Data
Baehr, Patricia Goehner.
The way to Windra.
Summary: Holly and Edward go through a mysterious
door that appears in Holly's room and find themselves
in the valley of Windra which is inhabited by elves
and where their eccentric great-aunt is queen.
[1. Fantasy]   I.   Owens, Gail.   II.   Title.
PZ7.B1387Way   [Fic]   79-23272
ISBN 0-7232-6179-2
Printed in the U.S.A. by Maple Press
Book Design by Kathleen Westray

FOR MY OWN
EDWARD

Contents

Aunt Margaret Matilda

"TAKE off your shoes by the door and give me your wet coats," Mrs. Randolf said, stepping back from the puddle that was forming under Holly's and Edward's feet. A thunderstorm had started suddenly while the children were walking home from school. "It's too bad Dad can't pick Aunt Margaret Matilda up at the bus depot. I hate to see her walk here in this terrible weather!"

"She's not here yet?" Holly asked, wringing one of her long brown braids and watching the water drop to the deepening puddle.

"No. And I can't imagine what is keeping her."

"Maybe she won't come," Edward suggested hopefully.

"She'd better come or your father and I won't be able to go on our trip."

"You won't be gone long," Edward said. "Holly and I could take care of ourselves."

"Don't be ridiculous! Either your aunt watches you this weekend or your father and I don't go to the mountains."

Mrs. Randolf left with their wet coats, and Holly and Edward sank glumly onto the couch in the living room. They had never met Aunt Margaret Matilda and didn't know quite what to expect. Neither of them were happy about having a total stranger come in to stay with them for three days.

"I know just how she'll look," Edward said. "She'll be as big as a giant, with a beak nose and the voice of a crow. Caw! Caw! Edward do this! Edward do that!" He began to dance around the room, flapping his arms and making raucous calls.

"She couldn't be anything like that," Holly argued. "After all, she is Dad's sister. How bad can she be?" Holly tried her best, but she couldn't convince herself, and she certainly didn't convince Edward, who had already devised plans to wear Aunt Margaret Matilda down if, as he put it, "she gives us any trouble."

Edward stopped his flight around the living room and fell into a chair. "How nice can she be with a name like Margaret Matilda? Normal people use only one name, and they would call themselves Maggie or Margie or ... or anything but Margaret Matilda. She's got to be weird!"

The doorbell sounded its loud ding-dong.

"You might as well answer it," Edward said gloomily. "No use in putting it off."

When Holly pulled the front door open, she stood eye to eye with a very tiny woman. "Good day," the woman said in a thin, crackling whisper.

Holly stared, speechless, at the sharp-featured face surrounded by tightly curled springs of dark-red hair, and two sparkling green eyes smiled at her. Beneath the eyes, a pointed nose jutted out rather strangely.

"Let Aunt Margaret Matilda in!" Mrs. Randolf called. "Don't leave her standing in the rain!"

"Thank you," Aunt Margaret Matilda said as Holly closed the door.

Mrs. Randolf gave the aunt a quick hug. "We appreciate your staying with the children. I'm sure they won't give you any trouble. Children! Come meet your aunt."

Edward slowly lifted himself out of the chair and walked up to his sister, who still stood dreamily by the door. "Come on. What's the matter with you?"

Holly didn't answer. The moment she had heard Aunt Margaret Matilda's soft voice, something had tingled inside, thrilling her as if someone had just decreed that school was outlawed or that from now on children would fly instead of walk. And yet, Aunt Margaret Matilda had said nothing particularly exciting.

"This is Edward. He's in the fourth grade, a cub scout, and he has just started playing the trumpet. Holly is . . . Holly! Stop your daydreaming and come here!"

Holly's head snapped up. "Oh, I'm sorry. I didn't hear you."

"This is our dreamer," Mrs. Randolf went on. "We think she may become a writer someday."

"Yeah, she's always imagining things," Edward added. Mrs. Randolf gave him a glance that meant, "That's enough from you!" Edward smiled innocently.

"All right. Holly, you take Aunt Margaret Matilda's coat, and Edward, you take the suitcase upstairs."

When Holly hung the coat in the closet, she noticed something unusual. Aunt Margaret Matilda had come out of the rain, but her coat was completely dry! There wasn't a drop of water on it. Holly was wrinkling up her nose in confusion as the front door banged closed and Mr. Randolf boomed, "I'm home!" He gave Holly a peck on the cheek.

"What's the matter, girl? We'll be home again in three days."

She smoothed her nose with her finger and smiled. "Nothing's wrong. I'm really happy that you and Mom are getting a chance to go away. I hope you have a good time."

"Is Aunt Margaret Matilda here yet?"

Holly nodded and pointed to the kitchen.

"In all probability, this is Aunt Margaret Matilda," Mr. Randolf said as he entered the kitchen.

"Is it possible that this is my brother?" whispered Aunt Margaret Matilda.

"I remember when I was little," Mr. Randolf explained to Edward and Holly who had followed him into the kitchen, "my big sister was always telling me how things were possible..."

"But not probable," Aunt Margaret Matilda finished.

Holly and Edward looked puzzled.

"You'll understand what I mean once you get to know this aunt of yours. With her, all things become possible."

Mrs. Randolf interrupted. "If we're going to make our train, we'll have to hurry."

The next half-hour was busy with packing a few extra things and last-minute instructions for Holly and Edward. After Mr. and Mrs. Randolf were on their way and the children were alone in the living room, Holly brought up the matter of Aunt Margaret Matilda's dry coat.

"Probably she had an umbrella," Edward suggested.

"She didn't. All she had was her coat and a suitcase."

"Maybe she walked with the suitcase over her head."

"Don't be silly. I saw her standing on the doorstep in the rain. Why wasn't her coat wet?"

Not having an answer, Edward said, "Stop imagining things."

"What is Holly imagining?" a high crackling voice asked. Aunt Margaret Matilda was carrying a tray of cookies. Jabbing one into his mouth and taking one in each hand, Edward related Holly's story of the dry coat to Aunt Margaret Matilda. "It's impossible," he finished, then licked around his lips to catch all the crumbs, and gave a satisfied grin.

"Does rain fall in a solid stream of water?" Aunt Margaret Matilda asked.

Edward thought for a moment and answered, "No, it falls in drops."

"In other words," she continued, "there are always spaces between the drops of water. Is that correct?"

"Sure. Everybody knows that."

"Isn't it possible that I could have walked between the raindrops?"

Edward bit on his top lip while he tried to think of something to say.

"It is quite possible, though highly improbable," Aunt Margaret Matilda finished, her sentence ending in a soft, cackling laugh. Then the tiny lady took herself out of the room in short, light steps.

"What do you think of that?" Holly asked.

Edward didn't answer her, for the thought had just occurred to him that perhaps Aunt Margaret Matilda had devised plans of her own to wear him down!

"It's quite possible that I shall enjoy having our aunt stay with us," Holly imitated.

"And it's highly probable that I won't!" Edward exclaimed.

A Mysterious Door

IN the middle of the night, Holly was awakened by the sound of a door closing. She opened her eyes and looked quickly around the room. Something very strange had happened!

Holly's room was small and square, with two doors and one window. Entering from the hallway, one saw a window seat to the right and the closet to the left. Holly's bed was on the wall that faced the door to the hall. There were a bookshelf, a rocking chair, and a bureau in the room, and on either side of the closet door hung embroidered pictures of animals.

Now, when Holly had opened her eyes and looked around the room, she saw a third door! It was next to the window, on the side closer to the bed. Holly squeezed her eyes closed and tried opening them again. The door was still there. Then she tried pinching herself to see if she was actually awake.

"If this really is a dream," she wondered, "would pinching wake me up? Or would I only be dreaming that I was pinching myself?"

Holly found no answer. The door remained. Leaning out from the bed to take a closer look, she saw that there was a space between the bottom of the door and the floor. From this crack shone a hazy yellow light.

"One thing is certain. That door can't lead outside because I can see through the window that it is still dark. Where can the light be coming from?"

Holly was afraid to get up and open the door, but she was very curious. After some deliberation, she decided to go over and take a closer look. "I don't have to open it," she reasoned. "What's the harm in looking?"

When Holly put her bare feet on the floor, she felt a cold breeze that seemed to be blowing from under the strange door. The breeze became a wind as Holly got closer. Her long white nightgown rustled against her thin legs, and her loose brown hair blew straight out behind her as she stood next to the door.

All this time Holly was hoping that the door was only a shadow and that she had imagined it. On other dark nights, she had been sure that all sorts of animals and monsters stood about her room, but each always turned out to be a coat, or a chair, or a shadow. That was what Holly had expected this door to be—"a figment of your imagination," as Mrs. Randolf was apt to say. But this is not what happened. The door was actually there.

Holly put her hand on the smooth doorknob. It was icy cold. Afraid that the door might somehow open, she removed her hand quickly, then noticed a keyhole. Had that been there before? She took a deep breath as she bent down to take a peek.

At first she could not make out anything. It was very bright on the other side of the door, and Holly's eyes were used to the dark of her room. After a few moments, though, she was able to recognize a landscape. It seemed that she was viewing everything from the side of a mountain. Below her, a river wove through a lush green valley, and in the distance stood tall mountains. Holly saw all of this in a moment's glance. She had not been looking for more than a few seconds when the worst thing imaginable happened. Just as Holly saw the faraway mountains, an eye looked back at her from the other side of the keyhole!

She gave a rather loud gasp and ran out of the room as fast as she could. "Help," she called. "There's a door in my room!"

Aunt Margaret Matilda rushed into the hall wearing a funny yellow polka-dot nightgown, and a sleepy Edward appeared a few seconds later.

"There's a strange door in my room," Holly repeated.

"You're joking," Edward grunted. He was not at all pleased to be roused in the night for some ridiculous invention of his sister's. If she had said there was a strange person in her room, or a strange animal, it would have been worth the trouble of getting up, but a door?

"Let's go into your room and see," said Aunt Margaret Matilda. She went into the little bedroom and turned on the light. Everything was as usual, with one window and two doors.

"There *was* a door right there only a few minutes ago," Holly insisted, pointing to the spot. "There was wind and a river, and mountains . . . and an eye!"

"She was dreaming," Edward said to Aunt Margaret Matilda, who was inspecting the wall next to the window. "Don't bother. She's always imagining things."

Holly glared at her brother.

"Come stay in my room for the rest of the night," Aunt Margaret Matilda whispered. She turned off the light and padded softly back down the hall. Holly followed, glad that she would not have to spend the rest of the night alone.

"Don't worry," Edward called after her in his best older-brother voice. "In the morning you will realize that it was only a bad dream."

But when the strong rays of the sun filtered through the frilly curtains of the guest room into Holly's eyes, the memory of her experience was vivid. The mysterious door, the landscape, and that eye! Could it have been a dream, she wondered? It seemed so real!

Holly entered her bedroom cautiously. Bright with sunlight, the room gave no hint of the adventure she had had or dreamed the night before. She dressed quickly then joined Edward in the dining room.

"Well, at least we won't starve," Edward greeted her. "Aunt Margaret Matilda is a good cook." He stuffed three layers of pancakes into his mouth. "Have any more nightmares?"

"No, and I don't believe that it was a nightmare."

"Don't tell me that you think a door appeared in your room and then disappeared?"

"I don't know what to think, Ed. All I know is what I saw."

Aunt Margaret Matilda brought out another stack of pancakes. "Just what did you see, Holly dear?"

"Are you saying that you believe her story?" Edward asked. "It's not possible."

"There are a great many things, Edward, that are improbable, but possible. I thought I told you that yesterday. Never say that something is impossible. You are bound to be wrong a number of times," Aunt Margaret Matilda warned.

Holly narrowed her eyes and stared at her aunt. "Do you really think that the door could have been there?" Her aunt nodded, and Holly continued. "There was light coming from under the door, and a freezing wind. I looked through the keyhole and saw a strange land. It wasn't anything like here. Then an eye looked back at me from the other side of the door. That's when I ran out." Thinking about that eye, Holly shivered. Who could tell what kind of creatures would dwell in that land beyond the door?

Aunt Margaret Matilda looked thoughtful and murmured, "Ah-huh!" Then, she stood up and announced that it was time for the children to leave for school.

"I've always wondered," Edward said on the walk to their school, "which side of the family you take after. Now I know."

Holly made a face. "I like Aunt Margaret Matilda. She's really very nice. She's . . ."

"Weird!" Edward finished.

They laughed. Aunt Margaret Matilda was certainly different from any of their other relatives, or, for that matter, any other adult that they knew.

"I know what you mean, Ed. She acts like she believes in the kinds of things that adults say are fairy tales. And, you know, I'm glad. It makes me think that maybe some of those fairy tales can come true."

When they reached the playground the children said good-by because they were in different grades and would not see each other for the remainder of the day. When school was finished, they met at the flagpole for the walk home.

Coming into the house, Holly called to Aunt Margaret Matilda, "We're home!" but there was no answer.

"I guess she went out. Let's have a snack."

They went into the kitchen, where two glasses of milk and a plate of cookies were waiting for them.

"She's a mind reader," Edward joked as he took the plate in one hand, the milk in the other, and walked into the family room to watch television. Holly followed with her glass of milk.

"How did she know we would want a snack when we came home?" she asked. "Don't you think it is odd that food would be waiting on the table for us? The milk is really cold, too. She knew just when we would be getting home."

"Don't be silly. We get home the same time every day, and why wouldn't we be hungry? You're exaggerating again. Why does everything become a mystery to you?"

There was a soft chuckle behind them.

"Aunt Margaret Matilda! How did you get in here?" Holly asked, her eyes wide.

"Yes, how?" Edward squinted his eyes. "You weren't in here when we came in. We would have seen you if you came through the door, and that's the only way into this room."

"Well, Edward, what are you suggesting?" the tiny woman asked, her voice trailing off in a soft laugh. "If I didn't come through the door, then I must have come through the wall."

"What?" the children shouted in unison.

Aunt Margaret Matilda smiled at them. "It is possible to walk through a wall," she said. "Let me explain it to you. Everything is made up of tiny particles called molecules."

"We learned that in school," Holly said, nodding.

"And, there are tiny spaces between these little molecules. Now, suppose that the molecules of my body line up with the spaces between the molecules of the wall. Wouldn't it be possible for my body to pass through the wall?" The children said nothing. "It is possible, but not probable," Aunt Margaret Matilda finished. "Anyone for more milk?"

Holly did her homework as quickly as she could so that she would have the whole weekend free. Then she climbed into the window seat in her room, drawing her legs close to her body and resting her head on her knees. She wanted some time to think about all the strange things that had happened in the short hours since her parents had left. First, there was the dry coat that came in out of the rain. Then there was the experience with the door, and, lastly Aunt Margaret Matilda's sudden appearance in the family room from nowhere. Edward didn't seem to make much of these things, but they bothered Holly. What if the door should appear again? How could she tell if it was real or a dream?

Holly decided to work out a plan with Edward— that is, if he would cooperate. She went into Edward's room, which was across the hall.

"Ed, could I talk to you for a minute?"

He was bent over his math homework, looking every bit like a martyr. As he glanced up, she began speaking rapidly.

"Don't say anything until I'm finished. Just suppose, for a minute, that a door really did appear in my room last night, and there really is another land on the other side of it. If the door should happen to appear again, I think someone should investigate. That's why I have decided to go through the door and explore the other land."

"You can't go by yourself," he protested, forgetting that he did not believe her story. "I'd better go with you."

"That's exactly how I felt," Holly said happily. "Now let's make some kind of plan so that I can call you if it happens tonight."

"Wait a minute! You've got me exploring some dumb, imaginary land with you!"

"It isn't imaginary. Please, Ed. What can it hurt? If nothing happens, you won't be any worse off."

"Oh, the silly games I play to make my little sister happy," Edward muttered. In fact, he thought the idea of another land terribly exciting, but he felt that at his age he shouldn't believe in such fairy-tale nonsense.

"How will I wake you?" Holly asked. "If I call, I might wake Aunt Margaret Matilda, and I don't want to leave my room because the door might disappear again.''

"That's a good point. How about if we rig up some sort of an alarm system from your room to mine?''

In the end, they decided to stretch a string between the two rooms. It would have to be done after Aunt Margaret Matilda had gone to sleep. One end of the string would be next to Holly's bed, and the other end would be attached to a small bell in Edward's room. If the door appeared, Holly would pull on the string, thereby ringing the bell and waking her brother.

For the rest of the evening, each time Holly and Edward looked at each other, a secret sharing smile passed between them. And Aunt Margaret Matilda smiled at them, as if she had her own secret, too. At eight-thirty, the aunt announced that she would be turning in early.

"I'll probably sleep as sound as a caterpillar in a cocoon!'' she chuckled. "Good night. Pleasant dreams!''

Edward had stored the string and bell in his room, and it took no time at all to install their alarm system. When it was rigged up, he said, "I only hope it works. We should have tried it out this afternoon. Now it would attract Aunt Margaret Matilda's attention. Well, you probably won't have to ring it anyway. Good night, Holly."

As soon as Holly had turned off the light, she jumped under the covers and stared at the place where the door had been the night before. She couldn't decide which would be worse—being disappointed if the door didn't appear, or really having it appear again! With that thought, Holly settled her head into the pillow and went to sleep.

Holly Rings the Bell 3

EDWARD was worried that the bell would not be loud enough to wake him, so he put it on his pillow, flattening the lumpy surface with his hand and laying the small silver bell in the hollow.

I'm sure to hear that, he thought, stretching out under the covers. First he tried sleeping on his back, then on his side, and finally on his stomach, but no matter which way he turned, he could not get comfortable enough to fall asleep. Switching on the light next to the bed, Edward reached out for a book. His hand came back with a nature book about snakes.

"The snake is a limbless scaled reptile," he read. The book began with information about the scientific classification of snakes. By the time he had read, "the suborder being called *Serpentes* or *Ophidia*," Edward's eyes had blinked shut. Even with the light in his room shining, Edward slept soundly until a few hours before dawn, when he was awakened by the sound of a bell. He jerked up into a sitting position and, remembering the alarm system, hopped out of bed. He tiptoed across the hall to Holly's room and peeked in. It was still dark. Edward could hear his sister's heavy breathing.

"Holly," he whispered hoarsely. There was no answer. She was asleep.

Disappointed, Edward went back to his room, only to see the bell lying on the floor next to his bed. He realized that he must have knocked it off the pillow in his sleep.

"Stupid bell! I don't know why I agreed to this silly plan of Holly's anyway. Nothing is going to happen."

He crawled under the covers and closed his eyes. There was a soft tinkle from beside the bed. "Stupid bell," he grumbled again. There was a second tinkling sound. Edward propped himself up and looked down at the floor. The last of the moonlight reflected the silver surface of the still bell.

Now Edward wondered if he was beginning to hear things. The bell sounded again, but this time he saw it move ever so slightly toward the door.

"Holly is pulling the string!" he gasped, and he ran back across the hall.

Holly was standing beside her bed, looking very pale in the dim room. "What took you so long? I was afraid that you weren't going to wake up!"

"Where is the door?" Edward asked, squinting his eyes and peering around the dark room. Holly pointed to the wall next to the window.

"It's really there! I can't believe it!" Edward exclaimed as the outline of the door became clearer.

"Maybe the next time I tell you something, you will believe me," Holly sniffed, her mouth pouting slightly. But Edward was more interested in the door than in apologies.

"Have you opened it yet?" he asked excitedly.

"No. Take a look through the keyhole."

Edward crept over to the large door, noticing how much colder the room became as he neared it. Crouching down, he saw the landscape just as Holly had described it. He muttered another "I can't believe it!" and reached up to twist the doorknob.

"Don't!" Holly gasped, grabbing his arm. "If we're really going in there, let's change our clothes first. I'm not going in my pajamas!"

"Well, all right," he agreed. "But hurry. The door might disappear."

Edward went back to his room, and Holly pulled open a dresser drawer. In half a minute, she was dressed in a pair of slacks, a blouse, socks, sneakers, and a heavy sweater. Edward appeared wearing jeans, a T-shirt, and cowboy boots.

"Don't you want to go back and get a coat or something? There's a cold wind coming under that door," Holly warned. She was beginning to wonder whether they should open the door. "Maybe we should leave a note for Aunt Margaret Matilda."

"There's not time for any of that. Look! The door is fading!"

The outer edges were becoming less sharp, and the light shining from under the door was dimming. Edward ran to the door. Maybe it's locked, he thought. He, too, was starting to worry about the wisdom of this adventure. Didn't Holly say that an eye looked back at her? Whose eye was it? Perhaps terrible monsters inhabited this land.

Holly grabbed the doorknob and twisted. "Help me, Ed. It's stuck!"

Forgetting their fears, both struggled to open the stubborn door. Rushing through the cracks under and above the door, the wind began a loud, almost human moan. With one terrific jerk, the children freed the mysterious door, and a powerful wind burst into the tiny bedroom. Holly's sheets began to flap and the curtains stood straight out into the room. The wind continued to roar around their ears.

"Come on!" Edward shouted above the wailing wind. The children grabbed hands and fought the strong air current to the door. Then the wind suddenly changed directions and sucked them through. They heard a loud slam behind them. The door was closed.

Everything died down and it was very quiet. Holly and Edward gazed around. A field of flowers stretched fragrantly out to a wide river. Behind them was the steep slope of a mountain. The door had vanished. The only living creature they saw was a bird circling high above them.

"Well, which way do we go?" Edward asked softly. It was so still that he was almost afraid to speak.

"I guess we should go down to the river. The mountain would be too difficult to climb," Holly said.

Being much too interested in their surroundings to talk, they began to make their way through the dewy grass. The flowers swayed in the early morning sunshine. From a distance, the river had looked smooth and sleepy, but when the children stood beside it, it gave quite a different appearance. The water rushed at an incredible speed without causing the smallest ripple. Edward thought that it would be impossible to swim across the wide expanse of water. The strong current would drag any swimmer far away downstream.

"It must be very deep," he said. "If there were rocks or anything close to the surface, there would be waves. I'll bet that the water goes down at least fifty feet! See how clear it is? But if you look right down to the bottom, you can't see anything for the darkness."

Holly leaned out over the water, trying to see the bottom.

"Be careful!" Edward shouted. "This river is dangerous. If you fell in, you wouldn't be able to fight that current. It would be the last I'd ever see of you!"

Holly tried to back up from the river's edge, but her feet had gotten firmly stuck in the mud. "Help me, Ed! I can't move!" She struggled to free herself. "Oh! And I think I'm sinking!" She was up to her shins in mud. "Please get me out. This must be quick*mud* or something. In no time at all, I'll be in up to my waist!"

"You're overdoing things again, Holly. You're

not sinking anymore. Grab my hand and see if you can step out." She held out both hands for Edward to take. He tugged as hard as he could until suddenly the mud gave way and both children sprawled to the ground. Edward rolled on the grass in hysterics.

After scraping the gooey earth from her shoes and slacks, Holly happened to look overhead to where a black bird was circling. "If I didn't know better, I would swear that that is the same bird we saw when we got here! Could it be watching us?"

"Don't be silly," Edward said, glancing up in time to see the bird fly away. "See? It's gone now. Haven't you imagined enough already?"

"Well, I certainly didn't imagine this place. This is real."

"I'm not so sure," Edward mumbled.

Before Holly had a chance to ask her brother what he meant, she was distracted by the sound of voices. "Are you sure this is the spot?" a gruff voice was asking.

"Of course I'm sure! I know these woods like the back of my wing," a rough, nasal voice answered sharply.

"Don't argue, please. Just look for them," a third voice said. Something about the quiet tone of the third speaker struck Holly. She wanted to see who the three people were, but she was afraid to move.

"It's all my fault, dear Queen. It was very stupid of me not to have realized," the gruff voice said.

"Everything will be all right when we find them," the third voice soothed. "It's not anyone's fault."

Suddenly, Holly knew why the voice had sounded familiar to her. She scrambled to her feet, and turned in the direction of the speakers.

"There they are," the high nasal voice said with relief when he saw Holly. "I knew I wasn't wrong."

Holly saw now that the rough, nasal voice belonged to a beautiful black crow, which sat on Aunt Margaret Matilda's shoulder. It was the largest crow she had ever seen. The gruff voice had come from a little man with a bristly brown beard. He was even shorter than Aunt Margaret Matilda! He had thick stubby legs and large feet. His hands seemed gigantic at the end of such short arms, and his fingers were knotted and covered with soft brown hair.

"I'll go collect some wood for a fire so we can cook some food, Your Highness," the little man said, bowing to his Queen before he disappeared into the brush.

"I'm going ahead to scout for giants, Your Majesty.

See you back at camp," the crow called as it fluttered into the sky.

Edward and Holly stood bewildered. "What are you doing here?" they asked their aunt.

"The door wasn't meant for you," Aunt Margaret Matilda explained. "It was meant for me."

"For you? But, why?"

"This is the Land of the Winds. Between the mountains lies a valley called Windra, home of the elves. I was born here. The Windrans decreed that I should be sent for because there is some sort of crisis. Tumbledum, the elf, was going to explain it all to me. They thought I might be of some assistance."

"Elves?" Edward repeated doubtfully.

"It was decided that Tumbledum should find me and bring me back to Windra. But when I was last here, I was only a little girl and Tumbledum mistook Holly for me!"

"It was Tumbledum's eye that looked back at me," Holly said, beginning to understand.

"Yes, and when you told me the story about the door, I knew that something was wrong in Windra."

"Wait a minute," Edward interrupted. "Why would the Windrans want you? And how could you have been born here? You're Dad's sister!"

Aunt Margaret Matilda smiled. "I am his half sister. You see, I am half elf."

The children gazed at her in disbelief.

"I can see by your faces that I will have to go back and start the story from the beginning. Make yourselves comfortable on that log, and while we eat I will tell you the story of my father, Charles Randolf, who was your grandfather, and how he came to Windra."

Aunt Margaret Matilda's Story 4

MANY years ago, there was a bold young man of twenty-five named Charles Randolf. He lived all alone in a tiny house on the edge of a wood.

While hunting one afternoon, Charles came across something very strange. There, in the middle of the wood, stood a door. Having hunted in that same place many times, Charles was sure that door had not been there before. He walked all around it but found only trees.

How odd, thought Charles. This door appears to lead nowhere.

Being a curious man, Charles turned the cold knob and opened the door. A tremendous gust of wind pushed him back, but Charles stood firm, and, holding tight to the door, he looked through its frame. On the other side, he saw a foreign landscape, much different from the wood he lived in.

If I don't go in, I shall wonder for the rest of my life what adventure I missed, he thought, and because he was always looking for excitement, Charles stepped through the doorway. In an instant, the door disappeared from behind him, and he was alone in the strange land.

Charles walked until he came to a wide river. He watched the water rush swiftly past him. All of a sudden, a section of the river began to swell, splashing water wildly. A huge glittering form rose from the swirling white waters, and Charles stood face to face with a gigantic river serpent! It had a head like a dragon's with huge nostrils, gleaming eyes, and a tremendous jagged mouth. The serpent's body was covered with gold scales, and Charles could see sections of the snake rising out of the water at different points in the river.

Charles stood perfectly still. He was afraid that the least little movement might cause the monster to reach out and grab him with its sharp teeth.

"Are you a live creature?" asked the serpent after a moment of silence.

Charles was so frightened that he was not surprised to hear the beast speak. "Yes," he answered meekly.

"You look quite odd to me," the serpent went on. "You are too tall to be an elf, but you are too short to be a giant. Just what sort of creature are you?"

"Why, I am a human, of course!" said Charles in surprise.

"A human! How exciting! Oh, I've heard that there were such things as humans, but I've never seen one. You must come from a different world. My world is called the Land of the Winds. This valley is Windra, where the elves live. The giants live in the Windsom Mountains. At first I thought that you were a small giant, in which case, I might have gobbled you up in an instant. I'm not too fond of giants. Well, it's lucky that I was clever enough to see that you aren't a giant!"

"Yes, I'm very fortunate," Charles said, noticing how the river serpent began to color a deep bronze, which Charles took for a blush.

"Oh, please don't think me conceited," the beast went on, "but, there are so many stupid serpents! Why, some of them have even been so dumb as to stray into your world!"

"Into my world?"

"Yes. I believe that you have called them Loch

Ness monsters, or some such name. Many creatures from The Land of the Winds have found
their way into your land."

"I guess that's where we get our legends about
elves, and giants, and ..."

"And Loch Ness monsters," the serpent giggled.
"Only now, you've discovered that we're not
legends. By the way, my name is Rupert Ophidia
Serpentes III. Do humans have names, too?"

"My name is Charles. May I call you Rupert for
short?"

"Certainly, Charles."

In no time at all, Charles and the serpent had
struck up quite a friendship.

"You'll stay with me tonight," Rupert said. "I
insist!"

"On the bottom of the river?" Charles asked.

"Yes. You'll like it. It's so quiet and dark. Perfect
for sleeping."

"I'm afraid humans can't live underwater,"
Charles explained. "We would drown."

"How awful! Well, in that case, I'll introduce
you to the elves. They're nice little fellows and I'm
sure they will be happy to put you up. Hop onto
my back and I'll take you downriver."

Rupert was careful to keep above the water the
section of his body where he carried Charles. The
serpent swerved through the fast current, splashing

and making huge waves. Charles had to concen-
trate on keeping his balance. He found the trip on
Rupert's back very like riding a wild, bucking
horse. The golden scales were hard and smooth,
leaving no place to hold onto.

A cluster of small buildings about half the size
of normal houses appeared. Made from long sticks
held together by mud, they were more like huts.

As Rupert stopped to let Charles off his back, a
crowd of stubby little men gathered. They stood
back, not sure whether the stranger was friendly.

"It's all right," Rupert called to them. "This is a
human. He has gotten into our world somehow,
and I thought you elves might be willing to put
him up for a while."

One of the elves stepped forward, and offered a
gnarled hand to Charles. "Welcome," he said.

"Thank you," Charles stammered, bending over
so that he was low enough to reach the elf's hand.
"My name is Charles Randolf."

"His name is Charles Randolf," was whispered
from elf to elf.

"I'm most willing to work for my keep," Charles
went on, gazing at the mass of pert faces intently
staring at him.

"He says he will work for his keep," echoed
hushed voices.

It was an awkward time for Charles. Everything

that he said was repeated through the elf crowd. Rupert was the one who finally put things at ease. "If I were one of you clever elves, I think I would take this stranger to the queen. She will be the one to decide if he can stay."

"The queen! Yes, off to the queen!" an elf shouted.

Another said, "I was just about to suggest that."

"I think we should take him to the queen," said someone else.

A chorus of little voices, all thinking the same thought, carried Charles away from the river bank. He turned and gave an uncertain nod of thanks to Rupert.

"Don't worry," Rupert called. "You'll get along fine. I'll stop by tomorrow to see how you're doing."

Charles looked like a sturdy oak in the midst of thorny bushes as he walked with the elves to the largest of the huts, which was nonetheless so small that Charles had to duck when he entered the low doorway. Inside, it was very dark. The elves knew their way, but Charles kept stumbling into pieces of tiny furniture. As he stooped to put a chair back into place, he noticed that the chair was carved in the likeness of an animal. When his eyes grew accustomed to the dim light, Charles was able to see that the whole room was filled with beautiful furniture. There was a round table that had a delicately carved pedestal depicting the history of the Windrans. Each chair around it was skillfully sculpted to resemble an inhabitant of the Land of the Winds. There was a serpent's face, an animal of some kind, an elf's head, and another large face with a frightening scowl. Charles thought that it looked almost human, and he asked what kind of being the chair represented.

"That's a giant," an elf answered.

Charles took a second look at the horrorful grimace and decided that he didn't want to meet up with any giants.

The elf who had first bid Charles welcome ushered him into a smaller chamber of the hut. There in the dim light, Charles saw the most beautiful carving of all. It was a woman. She was in perfect proportion, but very small. The features of her face were sharply carved but delicate. Long chestnut locks fell about her shoulders.

"Your Majesty, the stranger is here."

Charles gasped as he saw what he had taken to be a statue move. The tiny woman was alive!

"Come sit by me," the woman commanded.

Speechless, Charles obeyed.

"If you come in peace, you are welcome to stay

with my people. I have been told that you have offered to work for your keep. That will be appreciat-
ed. You are a large man and my people are unable
to do heavy work. You may be of help in the building of huts."

Gazing fondly into the queen's violet eyes,
Charles said, "Huts? I could build you a palace!"

The next day Rupert found Charles already hard
at work building a stone house on the river bank.

"Looks like you are planning to stay awhile,"
Rupert commented.

Charles smiled. "Yes, I am building a home for
Elisandra."

"You mean *Queen* Elisandra," the serpent
quickly corrected. "You must always speak of the
queen respectfully. Refer to her as Her Majesty,
Her Highness, or Queen."

"Oh, we had a long talk yesterday, and she has
asked me to call her Elisandra."

"You must have truly impressed her," Rupert
said.

"I'll let you in on a secret, Rupert, old boy, since
you are my oldest friend here in Windra . . ."

"We met only yesterday . . ."

"I am in love with the queen," Charles
announced.

Rupert fell back, almost submerging. "The elves

will not stand for it! You, a human from another world, and their Windran queen? Never!"

Despite Rupert's warning, Charles proceeded to court Queen Elisandra. By the time his stone house was completed, he had proposed marriage. And to everyone's surprise, she had accepted! Although they protested bitterly at first, the elves soon came around to their queen's side. As a rule, elves are not especially hard people to convince. The very elves who had said, "It's an abomination to think of a human marrying our queen," were soon saying, "Charles Randolf is the very man to wed our queen. Couldn't find a better man anywhere! The moment I saw him, I thought, Now there's a man to marry our queen!"

The couple was married in a traditional Windran wedding ceremony. Elisandra looked like a fairy-tale princess in a bridal gown of woven daisies. On her head, she wore a crown made from golden river-serpent scales. According to legend, if they were married on the back of a river serpent, it would bring the couple good luck, and Rupert was only too happy to oblige. The winds blessed the marriage and everyone was pleased.

The elves' wedding gift to the royal newlyweds was lovely carved furniture, much of it made in two sizes—small pieces for Elisandra and large ones for Charles. There were chairs, two tables, benches, chests, a huge four-poster bed with a feather mattress, everything needed to furnish the stone house royally. They settled into the house by the river and began their new life together.

In a year's time, a daughter was born to them, and they named her Margaret Matilda. Margaret was the name of Charles's mother, and Elisandra's mother had been called Matilda. The little girl grew to be a delightful combination of her parents. She had her father's clever mind and her mother's quick wit, and she looked just like an elf with a pointy nose and pixy face. One thing Margaret Matilda could never stand was being treated like the Windran princess she was. The elves made quite a fuss over her, bowing deeply whenever she passed by. When she complained about their behavior to her mother, Elisandra shook her head and told her to get used to it. "Someday, you will be the queen."

Margaret Matilda spent most of her time roaming about the valley. She and one of her friends, Tumbledum, took turns riding up and down the river on Rupert. The serpent was like one of the family. He picnicked with them on the river bank and told stories about the Windra of years gone by. It was a very happy time. Unfortunately, it was not meant to last.

When Margaret Matilda was ten years old, Elisandra took sick with the dreaded witch's plague, a horrible illness that turned the skin a purple-blue color. Despite the best care, the queen died. The entire valley mourned the loss of their beautiful and beloved ruler. Filled with grief, Charles decided that there was no longer any reason for him to stay in Windra, and he made plans to return to his own world with Margaret Matilda. The elves made an uproar. They forbid him to take their new queen away. Margaret Matilda was the only heir. Charles stood firm, saying that his daughter was too young to rule anyway. He was the father and he intended to do what he believed was right. Eventually, the elves gave in.

Before leaving, Charles helped to establish a new system of rule, whereby a head elf was elected every five years.

Charles and Margaret Matilda made their farewells to everyone. The saddest parting was with Rupert. "You are the best friend that I ever have had," Charles said. "I wish that you could come with us, but I know that it is not possible . . ."

"Please, Daddy, anything is possible!" Margaret Matilda pleaded.

"Not this time, I'm afraid."

"Don't cry," Rupert said with sparkling tears

running down his golden snout. "I know that we will meet again. Now, off with you both! The winds have opened a door to your world."

And so they went to Charles's world. It was many years later when Charles Randolf remarried. He and his new wife gave Margaret Matilda a brother, who was to become the father of Holly and Edward.

Off to the Elf Camp | 5

AUNT Margaret Matilda finished the story and gazed quietly into the fire, remembering times past.

"With trouble in Windra, the only one to turn to was our beloved queen." Tumbledum bowed low, his beard dipping into the campfire. "She is the only one who can help us now," he continued, as a wisp of smoke arose from his brown beard. Then, suddenly, an orange flame began to illuminate the elf's astonished face! He bowed up and down several times while muttering, "Excuse me, Your Highness. Most unfortunate, Your Majesty. I ... um ... please forgive this ... I beg your leave, Your Grace ..."

Holly jumped up and threw her sweater over the elf's head, and she and Aunt Margaret Matilda began to pat out the flames. After a few tense moments, the fire was extinguished and the sweater removed, revealing what was left of Tumbledum's smoldering beard. The little elf raised his knobby fingers to the place where his lovely full hair had been.

"My beard," he sniffed. His eyes filled with tears. Bowing, he left the group and disappeared into the trees.

Aunt Margaret Matilda started to put out the campfire, and Holly helped by throwing dirt over the charred wood. Edward, who sat apart, leaning against a thick oak, began to giggle, and the giggle soon became a shrill laugh.

"Just what do you find so amusing?" Aunt Margaret Matilda demanded.

"The . . . the elf!" Edward panted amid his hysterics. "He looked so funny! His beard . . . his . . . ah haha!" Gasping for air, Edward held his stomach and curled up on the ground, laughing.

Aunt Margaret Matilda stood with her hands placed firmly on her hips and a frown on her face. Holly ran to her brother and angrily cried, "Ed, you are mean! Tumbledum could have been badly hurt! How can you think that is funny?"

"Oh, leave me alone," he replied, regaining his

breath. "You don't seem to understand that none of this is real! It's all a dream. No one can get hurt in a dream."

"What are you talking about?"

"The last time I was awake was when I was reading in bed. Because I was thinking about your silly tale of a disappearing door and another land, when I fell asleep I began to dream this crazy dream. At first, I did think it was real, but after seeing a talking crow and an elf, and hearing stories about river monsters ... well, forget it! This has to be a dream."

"But, Ed, this is really happening! I know I'm not asleep, and neither are you. You've got to believe me!"

"Sorry, Holly. I don't believe you. Besides, the real you is asleep in bed. You're just the Holly of my dream."

"Well, young man," Aunt Margaret Matilda broke in, her voice soft, yet firm, "you had just better behave yourself in this dream, or you will find yourself in trouble when you wake up!"

Edward sobered at this. Aunt Margaret Matilda left him and joined Tumbledum, who had reappeared in the clearing. "Are you all right?" she asked.

"Yes, Your Highness." The sides of Tumbledum's beard had not been damaged, but the center section had burned almost to the skin. Fortunately, none of his face had been scorched. "If I may be so bold, dear Queen, I suggest that we head towards the elf camp," he said with all the dignity he could muster.

"Camp? What happened to the village?"

"We were forced to leave it . . . uh . . . due to that problem I started to tell you about . . ."

"Look here, Tumbledum. If the river has risen, or the land has gotten too marshy, I simply cannot do anything about it! You elves must learn to solve your own problems. That is what the head elf is for."

"Please, Your Majesty . . ."

"My responsibility is to my family. I promised that I would look after the children, and I can't go running about Windra . . ."

"Listen!" Tumbledum shouted. Aunt Margaret Matilda stopped in midsentence, her mouth frozen open. "I beg you to forgive my rudeness, but this is something much more serious. We were forced to leave the village by the giants. They have declared war."

"War? With the giants? That's unfair."

Holly came to her aunt's side. "What caused the war?"

"That's just it. We don't know. All we are sure

of is that the giants want us out of the Windran valley."

"Edward," said Aunt Margaret Matilda, "please come and listen. I am worried about my elf friends, and I would like to find out more about this war. What would you think if we stayed just long enough to see the head elf?"

"Great!" Holly said happily.

Edward shrugged. "It's okay with me. Then the dream will only be a bit longer."

Following Tumbledum's lead, the group hurried through the forest. There were no paths to follow, and Holly found it difficult to keep up the pace through the dense undergrowth. No one spoke. All energy was spent on traveling as fast as possible.

Holly found that she was constantly on the lookout for giants. How big would a giant be? Would one be taller than the trees? A thorn grabbed at Holly's pants leg, and she had to stop and untangle her clothing. When she caught up with the others, she found them crouching in the bushes, their eyes directed to a black crow circling overhead.

"Shhh!" Aunt Margaret Matilda warned, pulling Holly down to the ground.

"What's wrong?" she whispered.

"Giants!" Edward exclaimed gleefully.

Tumbledum put his boney hand over Edward's mouth and drew him closer to the dirt. On the other side of the bushes there was a soft rustling and the sound of twigs cracking under great weight. Holly drew a deep breath and held it. She only hoped that the loud thumping of her heart would not be heard by whatever stood just beyond the shrubs. Was there one giant, or was there a group? Holly flattened herself on the damp ground and peered through the leaves at the base of a bush. There, not more than four feet away, stood a giant! He was enormous! Holly estimated that he was at least ten feet tall and probably weighed a ton. His face had close-set small round eyes and a bulbous nose. His uneven black hair was arranged in knots. The giant scratched his stomach through the mangy animal pelts that were his clothes, and yawned. He turned all round, letting his eyes stop right on the bush where they were hiding! For a moment it seemed that they were going to be caught, but the giant turned and marched noisily away, humming a tuneless melody in his deep, bass voice.

Everyone remained perfectly still, wanting to be sure that the woods around them were no longer occupied. Tumbledum cautiously squinted over the bushes. "It's all right. The giant is gone."

"Gosh, I hope we run into another," Edward said. "I didn't get a chance to really see this one."

Tumbledum gave the boy a curious look and then shook his head, not bothering to question Edward's odd desire.

"Let's go!" Aunt Margaret Matilda commanded, and once again they were tramping through the thick green of the Windran woods.

It seemed to Holly that the forest was constantly getting darker. The trees overhead no longer let the sky show through. Up ahead, it appeared that there was a solid wall of green. As they came closer, Holly could see that it was made up of trees, leaves, bushes, vines, and hanging moss, vegetation so thick that it completely blocked any view farther into the woods.

"Here we are," said Tumbledum. The elf parted the flora as if it were a curtain, and they passed from the dim emerald green of the forest into a bright clearing bustling with tiny figures running every which way.

"There must be hundreds of elves," Edward remarked.

"Aren't they cute?" Holly giggled softly, taking care that Tumbledum didn't hear her. "Look at that little elf woman with her child! The baby is no bigger than one of my dolls."

"And look at that boy playing with the stick. He seems to be about our age, but he's only half our height."

Holly turned to ask Tumbledum a question about the game the elf children were playing, but the stubby man and Aunt Margaret Matilda had gone on to one of the tents. The children hurried after, following them through the green flap of the largest tent. Inside were three strange elves, nervously shuffling about before their queen.

"Welcome, Your Highness."

"Most honored, Your Grace."

"Uh, same for me."

The three knobby elves were bent at the waist, their small brown hats in their hands.

"I'll never get used to this," Aunt Margaret Matilda said under her breath. "Please sit down," she said to the elves.

"Your every wish is my command!"

"Oh, yes, dear Queen!"

"Uh, same for me."

After a few more quick bows, everyone was seated at a long wooden table.

"We are so relieved to see you, Your Majesty."

"Yes. We're counting on you to save the valley."

"Uh, yeah."

The three looked almost identical. Each had a

long silver-white beard and bushy eyebrows that moved up and down as he spoke. Holly noticed that they always spoke in the same order, and she began to think of them as Elf One, Elf Two, and Elf Three.

"Which one of you is the head elf?" asked Aunt Margaret Matilda.

"We all are," they said in unison.

"If I may explain?" Elf One asked. "You see, Your Highness, last election, my two brothers and I ran for the position of head elf. The Windrans were unable to decide who to elect, so we thought it would be easier if all three of us took the job."

Elf Two nodded his head vigorously, and Elf Three added, "Uh, that's right!"

"What are you doing about this war with the giants?"

"I think that we should attack them at their settlement near the river," said Elf One, pounding his fist on the table.

"I think that we should wait until they attack us, and then defend ourselves!" said Elf Two, clenching the edge of the table tightly.

"Uh, I think that we should avoid fighting at all costs, and, uh, just leave Windra," said Elf Three.

Then they began to fight among themselves, arguing over whose plan was the best.

Aunt Margaret Matilda stood up and, summoning all of her dignity, said, "I command that you stop this bickering!"

Immediately there was silence in the tent. Even Edward and Holly drew back into the darkness of the corner. An angry queen was a fearful sight!

Her face fiercely set, Aunt Margaret Matilda boomed, "How can you attempt to rule Windra when you can't even agree among yourselves?"

In an effort to please their queen, the three elves smiled and cleared their throats.

"We can agree on certain things," ventured Elf One.

"Oh, yes," affirmed Elf Two.

"Uh, it's true," said Elf Three, and then he turned to his brothers and asked, "Like what?"

There were several uncomfortable moments while the elves struggled to think of something that they could agree on. Finally Elf One spoke. "I think that we should have a celebration tonight to welcome our queen back to Windra."

"I agree with that suggestion."

"Uh, so do I."

With that, the head elves scurried off to proclaim the news to the rest of the camp.

Aunt Margaret Matilda called the children to her side. "I know we really shouldn't stay, but how can we leave now?"

"We can't leave them," Holly agreed. "We must

stay and try to help."

"What do you think, Edward?"

"Why not? This is the best dream that I've ever had!"

"I guess it's settled. We'll stay tonight, and during their celebration I'll meet with the elder elves and see if we can't come to some solution. Tomorrow morning, bright and early, it's back to our own world. Remember, your parents will be home tomorrow night!"

Celebration for a Queen | 6

WHEN Aunt Margaret Matilda, Holly, and Edward came out of the meeting tent, they were met by the entire elf camp, everyone pushing forwards to get a glimpse of the queen. Aunt Margaret Matilda smiled and announced that she would see them all.

"Make a line," she commanded, "and I will say hello to each of you in turn."

Having forgotten how her subjects would behave, the queen sighed deeply as the line began to file past her, each elf bowing several times. All the while that the little people were in sight of their ruler, they showed their respect by bending at the waist. Everywhere Holly and Edward looked, they saw elves bobbing up and down like one tremendous playground of seesaw riders. Finally, the elves went back to their work. There was much to be done for the evening's celebration.

Aunt Margaret Matilda, the head elves, and the elders returned to the meeting tent, and Holly and Edward were left to wander around the site. The cooks were preparing a soup for the dinner, cutting up odd-looking roots and dropping them into a huge cauldron that bubbled over a fire. A tiny pixy-faced woman seemed to be the head chef. "You go and find more nim roots," she said to one wizened elf. "And you skin the rabbit for the soup," she ordered another. "Did anyone put in the moss-covered rock?"

"I don't think we should watch them make the soup if we are going to eat it," Edward said as velvety-green coated stones dropped into the cauldron with a loud plop-plop. "It's better that we don't know what's in it."

"Oh, look," Holly said, hurrying over to the edge of the camp where a large black bird was preening himself. "It's the crow we met in the woods. Hello! Was it you who warned us about the giant?"

The crow shook himself and then smoothed his

feathers. "Was me," he said. "No need for thanks. All in the line of duty, you know."

"What's your name?"

"Suka. S-U-K-A. Suka. I can read and spell as well as talk."

Holly noted how proudly the crow spoke. "My, that's remarkable," she said flatteringly.

Edward looked unimpressed. "Can you write?" he asked.

The crow cleared his throat and fluttered his wings. "How would you suggest I hold the pen, boy? With my feet? And fly around to move it?"

Edward shrugged. "Sorry. I was just wondering."

"I suppose I could do it if I really tried," Suka mumbled.

"Are there many talking animals?"

"I should say not, Holly-girl! There used to be quite a few, but I'm the only one I know of now. Those dratted head elves botched up all the magic around here when they took over. I guess the winds don't like them."

"Aunt Margaret Matilda mentioned the winds in her story. Who, or what, are they?"

"They're everything! They blew this valley and the Windsom mountains together. They give it its magic. They're always up there—watching what happens."

"Are they good or bad?"

"Well, good I guess. Unless you've done something wrong! Then, watch out!"

Holly shivered as she felt a breeze run past her head. Was that one of the winds?

Edward looked the crow over carefully. "What magic can you do?"

Suka hopped a few times on the branch where he stood. "Magic? Me? Well . . . I can talk, and . . . I can fly."

"All the birds in our world can fly," Edward said plainly.

"Can you?" Suka squawked loudly. He was a conceited crow.

"No," Edward admitted, "but there are birds in our world that can talk, too. Lots of them. Why, in the pet store around the corner from our house, there is a parrot that can say, 'Polly want a cracker?' Isn't that right, Holly?"

"Not exactly. It doesn't know what it is saying. That's not the same as Suka, here, who really thinks and talks . . . and reads!" she added at the last moment. She watched Suka regain his composure and puff out his feathers.

"That's not the same, indeed!" the crow said.

Edward gave Suka a sour look. "Oh, what's the difference? You're not real anyway." With that, he walked to the other side of the camp.

"What was that he said? Not real? I'm real! I'm real!" cawed Suka, and Holly began to think that he did sound very like that parrot in the shop around the corner from their house.

"Don't pay any attention to Edward. He's not usually like this. It's only that he thinks he's dreaming."

"You mean asleep?"

"Yes. He thinks that nothing matters because we're all part of his dream."

Suka made a cawing sound. "That could be dangerous. He could get into trouble believing that he is in a dream and can't get hurt. But don't worry. Suka's on duty. I'll keep an eye on him."

The afternoon passed interestingly enough for Holly and Edward, but there was nothing but problems in one of the tents.

"We've got to face facts," an elder elf was saying. "Giants against elves just isn't fair. I still vote with Duff to leave Windra."

A few elves cheered, but others raised their voices in dissent. "I'll never leave Windra!" one red-haired elf vowed.

"Quiet! Quiet!" Aunt Margaret Matilda protested. "I've heard enough. I can't see giving up Windra when we don't even know why the giants want us out. The first thing to do is find out why we are fighting. When we have that answer, we'll know what to do. Perhaps we can work out some sort of compromise."

No one dared argue with Aunt Margaret Matilda, and whether anyone disagreed was never found out because a queen's word was law.

"We will adjourn for dinner," Aunt Margaret Matilda announced. The elves silently filed out of the tent.

The sky grew dark quickly as the sun disappeared behind the Windsom Mountains. Soon there was just the soft glow from the cooking fires and, in the camp's center, one bonfire around which everyone sat. The first course was the soup that Edward and Holly had seen being made. They forgot the strange ingredients with the first mouthful.

"This is delicious," Edward said, slurping the soup from a carved spoon. "Have you tried a piece of the nim root?"

Holly poked around in her bowl until she found the spongy root. "Ummm. It melts in your mouth!"

The rabbit meat gave the broth a wild flavor, and the nim added a foreign, spicy taste. It was unlike anything the children had ever tasted.

The next course was baked potatoes and stuffed venison. Each chunk of meat was slit and filled with a mixture of mushrooms and crab apples. The fruit penetrated the meat, flavoring and tenderizing it. Off to the side of the fire were two large bowls. One was filled with assorted greens and the other contained a Windran specialty: blueberry wine.

After the wine had been served in wooden goblets, Aunt Margaret Matilda motioned for the ceremonial dance to begin. Ten young elves dressed in colorful, flowing robes came out into the circle. There were several very complicated steps followed by deep bows. They moved around the bonfire as its flames licked the night sky, each elf stepping and bowing in time to rhythmical taps made by hitting a stick on a hollow log.

After the dance, Aunt Margaret Matilda and the elders left the group to continue their meeting. Holly began to think that the evening was over, but then the elves started to call, "Tumbledum! Tumbledum! Tell us about your adventure with the winds!" Throughout the evening, Tumbledum had sat apart from the rest, hiding his charred beard, but when the chanting began, two strong elves dragged their friend to the center of the circle. Everyone clapped, and Tumbledum made an embarrassed bow to his audience.

"It was on an eerie Windran night like this that

I nearly met my end," he started, and turned to face Holly and Edward, the elf's face shadowed in the firelight, looking like a skull.

"There are three winds here. The Valley Wind is a gentle breeze that blows milkweed seeds across the meadow and makes the leaves whisper to the sky. The River Wind is a wild wind. Untamed, it bends the trees to the earth and races over the land. The Mountain Wind is the strongest, and it can tear tall oaks from the ground and rip them apart! All the winds are magical, but the Mountain Wind has the most powerful magic." The leaves rustled in the otherwise still night air, and the listeners shivered.

"That moonless evening, I lost my way in the darkness. I stumbled into a clearing that I had never seen before. There I saw a sight that was for no elfin eye to behold. It was a gathering of fairies . . . delicate fairies dancing around in a circle. One of the winds was there, too, gently lifting the fragile dancers up and down. I was enchanted, and I remained behind a tree, watching them until one little fairy turned and spied me! 'Look,' she cried in an almost inaudible whisper. 'An elf is watching us!' Another fairy called, 'Take care of that peeping elf, Mountain Wind!'

"When I realized that it was the powerful

Mountain Wind, the spell was broken. I turned and began to run for my life! Crazed, I bumped into trees and stumbled over roots, never stopping because I could hear the wind blowing in the woods behind me, the sound coming closer by the second. All of a sudden, the wind was roaring around my ears and I was blown to the ground. I covered my head with my hands as the wind tossed stones at me. I knew that if I stayed much longer, the stones would get larger and larger until they crushed my skull! Drawing a deep breath, I sprang from the dirt and started to run again. The wind stayed at my side and I realized that it was useless. 'Leave me be,' I pleaded, but in the wind's deafening howl, my voice was lost. Suddenly, I had the strangest sensation. I felt light. My legs had stopped running, but I continued to move forwards. In the dim starlight, I saw that I was floating through the air! High into the night sky, up past the mountain peaks, I flew, up, up, and still up—so high that I didn't believe I would ever see the earth again. For a moment, I stopped, suspended above Windra, only to start a spiraling tumble down again! Faster and faster I fell. It was now clear that the Mountain Wind had taken me high into the sky to drop me to my death! But when I was only moments from crashing into the ground,

I was lifted in a gentle pocket of air. It was the Valley Wind! I was floated slowly to the ground and set down lightly. Seeing what had happened, the Mountain Wind came rushing at me, but then the River Wind met it, and the two began a terrific struggle. There were loud crashes of thunder, and the sky was ablaze with spears of lightning. Taking the opportunity the River Wind had given me, I ran for the village. The Valley Wind stayed at my back, seeing me safely home."

The elves clapped their bony hands joyfully. They had heard the tale many times, but they enjoyed it more with each telling. Tumbledum was beaming. He bowed to all sides. Then, remembering his singed beard, he blushed, covered his bare chin, and left the circle.

Aunt Margaret Matilda came from the meeting tent, followed by the elders.

"Ahem," said Elf One to get everyone's attention. "Her Majesty, Queen Margaret Matilda of Windra, daughter of Queen Elisandra, granddaughter of Queen Matilda, great grand-daughter of . . ."

"Has a speech to make," interrupted Elf Two.

"Uh, yes," said Elf Three. "Uh, here she is!"

The camp was silent as the queen addressed them in her whispery voice. "Dear Windrans. It is quite probable that this will be the last time I will speak with you." Holly immediately added under her breath, "But possibly not!" although she did not know why she had such a thought.

"Tomorrow morning," the queen continued, "I will be leaving with my niece and nephew to take them back to their own world." There were many sighs from the elves. "Do not worry. I am sure that the head elves will be able to handle matters here. We have been in conference and, together, have decided upon courses of action. To begin with, a delegation will be sent to speak with the winds. One thing is firm: We will not give up Windra."

A cheer went up all around. Even Elf Three, who had wanted to leave, cheered. By this time, he thought that it was his idea to stay and fight.

"Isn't that great, Ed?" said Holly, turning to look at her brother. But he was not beside her. She quickly searched the area, then, frantic, she interrupted the royal speech.

"Aunt Margaret Matilda! Edward's gone!"

The Cave of the Winds | 7

ALL night a wind howled in the elf camp. Under a blanket in a tent with Aunt Margaret Matilda, Holly listened to the canvas flap in the gale.

"That must be the River Wind—so wild and noisy," she thought. "I do hope Edward is all right."

Edward had not turned up in the late-night search conducted by the elves. Aunt Margaret Matilda theorized that he had gone off into the forest, assuring Holly that he would be all right. Still, Holly worried.

The morning was sunny and bright. Holly remembered that it would be Sunday morning back in her world, and her parents would return from their weekend holiday that evening. Would Edward be found in time? As she came from the tent, she heard many birds singing their morning songs. One of the voices was nasal and rough. It was Suka.

"The crow is the best bird of all!
He has a special call—
Caw, Caw, Caw, Caw,
The crow is the best bird of all.

"And Suka is the best of the crows
'Cause he can say what he knows.
Caw, Caw, Caw, Caw,
Suka is the best of the crows!"

"That's a very nice song, Suka."

"Oh! Good morning, Holly-girl. Thank you. I wrote that song myself." The crow hopped happily on his branch, and each corner of his beak seemed to turn up in a smile.

"Have you heard anything new about my brother?"

The corners of the beak dropped. "No. Are you mad at me, Holly-girl?"

"Why should I be?"

"I promised to look after your brother . . . and now he is lost."

Holly stroked the glistening blue-black feathers on Suka's head. "It's not your fault. He took it upon himself to leave."

"I'm going to be the one to find him," Suka vowed, and, with a flutter, he was off into the trees.

Holly found her aunt beside the charred remains of the bonfire, organizing search parties. "The three head elves will each lead a group of ten men. One group will head towards the river, one group will go inland along its course, and the third will head back towards the mountains. Any questions?"

"What if we run into some giants?" one of the elders asked.

"Hide," the queen ordered. "I don't want anyone getting hurt. If a giant sees you, run. You're small enough to escape into places where a giant can't fit."

"What if we see the boy and he is a prisoner of the giants?"

"Don't try to rescue him. Come back to camp and report it to me. If there are no more questions, I think that the parties should set out. Be back here before nightfall."

"Aunt Margaret Matilda, is Edward really safe?" Holly asked as the elf army marched off into the forest.

"That, Holly dear, is what I am going to find out. While the elves are searching, I am going to visit the winds."

"How?"

"They live in a cave in the tallest of the Windsom Mountains. I've never been there, but I think that I can remember the secret directions."

"Let me come with you. Maybe I can help you find it."

"It might be frightening. Are you sure?"

Holly nodded.

"All right, then," Aunt Margaret Matilda said. "Let's gather some provisions and get going."

They fashioned a back pack and filled it with food, a canteen of water, a rope, and a curious carved stick on a string. Aunt Margaret Matilda strapped the pack over her shoulders, and they started off through the dense undergrowth, keeping the mountain range before them. It was a long, hard walk, but when the sun was directly overhead, they found themselves at the foot of the tallest mountain.

"We will stop here for lunch," Aunt Margaret Matilda decreed. "We'll need the rest and nourishment for the climb up the trail."

Holly looked at the mountain and saw a ribbon of gray winding up and up! It was at about the same angle as the slide in her school playground! She had enough trouble trying to climb that—how could she climb the mountain? It was so much taller, and it looked dangerous.

After they had finished the venison left over from the night before and had washed it down with the water, Aunt Margaret Matilda stood erect at the foot of the trail. "Naaa, naaaa," she called up at the mountain, cupping her hands around her mouth to amplify the sound. "Naaa, naaaa!" For a moment it seemed as though nothing was going to happen. Then, there was the sound of pebbles and stones falling, and a furry head poked out from behind a rock. It was a goat. "Naaa," it answered the queen.

"Hello. We would like to go up the path to the cave of the winds."

"Naaa," said the goat.

Aunt Margaret Matilda scratched her cheek in puzzlement. "We would like to use your help in getting up the mountain."

The goat only said, "Naaa."

With a sigh, she turned to Holly. "It appears that this is not a talking goat. I don't know what has happened to the magic around here, but I hope the winds are home."

"Look! Even though that goat can't talk, it seems to understand you," Holly said, pointing to where two goats now stood.

Aunt Margaret Matilda helped Holly onto the back of the second goat. Taking the rope from her back pack, she tied Holly securely onto the animal's back. "The trail is pretty steep," she explained. "I don't want you falling off."

Aunt Margaret Matilda leaned over the first goat, struggling to get seated. Finally, the goat placed its head under her and gave a gentle shove. She was up.

"Thank you," she said, giving the goat a pat between its horns. Then she grabbed hold of the horns and said, "Let's go!"

The sure-footed beasts began the ascent. Sometimes the slope was so steep that Aunt Margaret Matilda almost fell off. Holly was glad to be tied on. Two times the goats had to leap from one jagged rock to another. But the scariest thing was looking down.

"How much farther?" Holly called ahead to her aunt after two hours of climbing.

"I don't know. We're almost to the top now. Maybe that's where we are going."

Sure enough, when the goats reached the summit, they stopped to let their passengers dismount. Feeling very sore, Holly and Aunt Margaret

Matilda climbed to the ground. Immediately, the goats ran off!

"Wait! Don't go! We'll never get down by ourselves!" Aunt Margaret Matilda called. She turned to Holly and sighed. "It's too late. They can't hear me."

She lowered the pack and took out the intricately carved stick. Holding the string, she let the stick dangle and watched it twist and spin about.

"What is that?" Holly asked.

"It's the royal scepter. It should show us to the cave of the winds." The stick stopped turning and pointed to a wall of rock.

"I don't see any entrance to a cave. Maybe the stick is wrong," Holly said.

"Possible but not probable. It looks as though we shall have to use some Windran magic. Do you remember when I told you about spaces between molecules, and walking through walls? Well, I was able to do that because all the things in the Land of the Winds, including the people, have larger spaces between the molecules. Our molecules are not tightly packed like yours. With concentration, and a little magical help, we are going to try and walk through this wall of rock. The cave of the winds must be on the other side."

"But suppose my tightly packed molecules can't make it through—is it dangerous?"

"I don't know for sure," Aunt Margaret Matilda confessed. "But I was able to do it in your world through the compressed molecules of the wall, so I can't see why you shouldn't be able to do it here with your molecules through this Windran wall with its loosely packed molecules. If you're afraid to try it, you can wait out here."

"I'll try," Holly said bravely. "What do I have to do?"

"Get as close as you can to the rock. Put your face right up against it. Good. Now, close your eyes and think about your molecules separating and making big spaces. Start to press into the stone. Keep thinking! Do you feel the rock molecules starting to line up with your spaces? Press into the rock. Keep pushing!"

"I'm trying, but nothing seems to be happening," Holly said, but as she spoke, she heard the quality of her voice change, and the word 'happening' echoed several times. When she opened her eyes, she found herself in a dark cave beside Aunt Margaret Matilda. She spit some pebbles from her mouth.

Her aunt laughed. "You shouldn't have talked. You opened your mouth right into the rock. Other than that, are you all right?"

"I'm fine," Holly said, flicking a stone from beneath her fingernail. "Is this the right cave?"

The answer came as a gust of wind. "Who has come to see the winds?" it howled softly.

"It is I, Queen Margaret Matilda, and my niece Holly."

"Welcome Windran queen. Enter the throne cave." Assisting, the wind blew them forwards through a narrow passageway and into a large cavern. Brightly colored stalagmites and stalactites reached from floor and ceiling. The sound of water trickling down stony walls echoed through the expansive cave.

Aunt Margaret Matilda turned to face a curious formation of greenish limestone that was the throne of the winds. There were three sections, one for each of the winds, and rising from each part were wide spears of limestone with many holes of all sizes and shapes. They looked much like long thin slices of green Swiss cheese. Holly found out later that it was a wind blowing through these holes that made the howling speech. Each hole produced a different language sound.

"We have come to find out what has happened to the boy, Edward, who disappeared from the elf camp last night," Aunt Margaret Matilda said, and her voice sounded hollow and weak in the damp cave.

"He is safe now," answered a wispy, high-pitched voice. "I am the Valley Wind, and I watched over him last night."

"Thank you," the queen sighed.

"We have waited many years for you to return, Queen of Windra," howled the powerful low voice of the Mountain Wind. "Nothing can be right in the Land of the Winds without a queen ruling the valley."

"The head elves are doing their best."

"They are fools!" the Mountain Wind said angrily. "They will ruin the valley."

"But every five years a new head elf will be elected," Holly said in defense of the little men, who she thought were cute.

A new voice started. It was whining and had an edge of laughter in it. "Every five years? Haven't you heard? Those elves have decreed that since there are three of them they should be in office for fifteen years!" With that, the voice began a fit of hysterical laughter.

"Who are you?" asked Holly.

"I'm the River Wind," it said. "Did you hear that? Fifteen years!" Once again it began to howl with mirth.

"Stop that," ordered the Mountain Wind. "If you don't stop, I shall send a hurricane to you."

The River Wind quieted down, but every once

in a while it would break into a few giggles.

"What has happened to the magic in the Land of the Winds? I've only seen one talking beast— And the giants! Why are they attacking? Why don't they stay in the mountains where they belong?" Aunt Margaret Matilda's voice quivered with emotion. "Nothing is right here."

"We have taken away almost all of the magic because we are unhappy with the head elves. There will be no more magic until a queen sits on the throne."

"Will you stay?" asked the Valley Wind.

"I've always missed Windra," Aunt Margaret Matilda smiled. "Ever since I left as a child, I've never been truly happy until yesterday when I returned. Even with the trouble of a giant war, I know that this is where I belong. Yes, I'll stay. But first I shall have to take my niece and nephew back to their world. Then I will return."

"Hooray!" shouted the River Wind.

"Where is my brother?" interrupted Holly.

"He really got himself into a fix," the River Wind chortled. "He was nearly a goner!"

"What happened?"

"Come closer to the throne. Look into the pool of water, and we will show you what Edward has been doing. You will also find out why the giants are attacking."

Holly and Aunt Margaret Matilda peered into the clear liquid. At first they saw only the pebbles under the water, but soon shapes began to appear.

"Can you see him?" asked the Valley Wind. "There he is, waking up from his night's rest next to the river."

Windran Gold | 8

EDWARD stretched and brushed the pine needles from his clothes. Was he still in his dream? It certainly looked that way. When would he wake up? He splashed some water from the river on his dirty face, smearing the grime from one part to another. He could hear low voices speaking somewhere close by, and he began to walk slowly in that direction. Two giants stood still, looking down into the river. They did not see Edward.

"Is this the right part of the river?" asked a blond-haired, cross-eyed giant.

"Yes," the other giant answered, rubbing a hand through his greasy hair. He was broad and flabby, and his clothes were coming apart at the seams. "When the sun reaches a certain point in the sky, it will light up the river so that we can see all the way down to the bottom."

"Oh, boy," said the blond giant, clapping his hands together greedily.

Wanting to see whatever it was that the giants had come to see, Edward went over and stood beside them, and he, too, peered into the dark waters. The giants were so preoccupied they didn't notice him. And Edward had no fear of these huge men because he still believed that he was dreaming.

"It should be any minute now."

As the sun came into position, its rays began to light up the river. First, it spotlighted the little fish, who, unused to the brightness, darted to the shadows. Next, they could see the vivid green plants that grew out from the river's side. When the sunlight finally rested on the bottom, the watchers had to cover their eyes. Cautiously, they squinted another look. The river bottom was brilliant with a glowing gold brightness!

"Gold!" Edward cried out. "There's gold on the bottom of the river! Thousands—no millions of dollars worth of *gold*!"

Startled, the two giants spun about and grabbed Edward before he had a chance to move. Valiantly, the boy squirmed in their solid grasp. "Let me go,

you overgrown bullies!" Edward managed to plant
a foot into the blond-haired giant's stomach.

"*Ooofff*! Why you little runt! What were you
doing, spying on us?" he glowered with crossed
eyes.

"Now I know why you want the elves out of
Windra. You want to steal the gold. The valley be-
longs to the elves. You belong in the mountains,"
Edward challenged.

"That information won't do you any good," said
the other giant. "You'll never live to tell anyone!"
With that, he picked up a length of rope that was
lying on the ground next to a sack he had been carrying. The blond-haired giant held Edward with
his arms pinned to his body while the other
wound the rope round and round Edward until he
could not budge. There was still some rope left
over, and this the giant tied to a large boulder.

"It doesn't matter what you do to me," Edward
sneered, "because this is my dream, and I won't let
anything harm me."

"Oh, really?" laughed the giants. "Well, see how
you like this!" One giant picked up the boulder,
and his friend lifted Edward. "One! Two!
Threeeee!" they shouted, and threw Edward tied
to the rock into the river! Edward went up into the
air, hearing the laughter of the giants and then the
plop of the boulder as it fell into the swift water.

He followed close behind with a splash. There was a loud gurgling noise and afterwards silence. Edward and the huge mass of stone began sinking to the river bottom.

A school of curious fish gathered around Edward, who was completely helpless. He exhaled, and a stream of rising bubbles scared the fish away. Left alone, Edward calmly observed the underwater sights. At first the water was clear, and Edward could see all around, but as he fell deeper into the water, it grew dimmer, and everything was tinted a murky green. Plants took on a dark, mysterious quality, and it even seemed that one reached out to grab Edward as he dropped past it. The eyes of a deep-water fish blinked open and shut next to him; then it swam away. Deeper and deeper Edward sank. Below, he could see nothing. The bottom was hidden in blackness.

Edward began to feel frightened. He couldn't breathe. Why didn't he wake up? If it was a dream, he would be able to breathe! Edward tried to take a gulp of air, but all he got was a mouthful of water.

The falling seemed endless. Edward sank into the dark water and could see nothing—not even when he looked down for his feet. He was starting to panic! He couldn't go without air any longer!

After that, Edward was not sure of anything. It seemed to him that he landed on the bottom of

the river, and a tremendous eye, more than a foot in diameter, blinked open. The river bottom began to move, as if there were an earthquake. Everything was churning! Something grabbed Edward and surrounded him. At that point, the boy passed out.

"Are you all right?" a voice asked. Edward choked and spit up some water. Taking a deep breath, he tried to put together what had happened. He was lying on the river bank, and a bright shape was hovering over him.

"I'm okay . . . I guess. Who are you?" He struggled to focus his eyes.

"You see, I was sleeping on the bottom of the river, and you woke me up—but that's all right because it was time for me to wake up anyway. I've been asleep for twenty years."

"I don't believe it! A genuine river serpent! I was rescued by a river serpent!" The beast colored an embarrassed bronze. "Isn't twenty years an awfully long time to sleep?" Edward asked.

"Oh, no, not for a river serpent. You see, we live for hundreds of years. I'm not even five hundred yet. Every hundred years or so, I need a few decades of sleep. Am I correct in thinking that you are a human?"

"Yes."

"I thought so. You remind me of Charles Randolf, a human who was here forty or fifty years ago."

"He was my grandfather. My name is Edward Randolf. Are you Rupert?"

"Yes! Oh, I say! How exciting. I'm so glad you dropped in on me!"

Edward grimaced, thinking how he had almost drowned.

"I might have simply gone back to sleep if I hadn't remembered something that your grandfather told me on the first day that I met him. He said that humans couldn't live underwater. You looked to me as if you might be a human, so I rescued you."

"Thank you," Edward said politely.

"Would you excuse me for a minute? I haven't had a bite to eat in years, and I am simply famished!" Rupert ducked under the water and came up with a fish in his mouth. "So, tell me what's new in Windra."

"The elves are having a war with the giants."

The serpent smacked his lips. "Oh, that's bad. Tsk, tsk. They haven't got a chance. Why did the giants come down from the mountains, anyway?"

"There's gold on the bottom of the river," Edward explained. "Gold is worth a lot of money. The giants want to drive the elves out of the valley so that they can have the gold for themselves."

"Gold," Rupert repeated. "And to think that I was sleeping on a fortune! That gold doesn't belong to the giants."

"Right. It's in the valley, so it belongs to the elves."

Rupert frowned. "No, it doesn't. It's in the river, so it belongs to me!"

Edward agreed. "I suppose you're right. And you certainly are capable of fighting off any greedy giants . . . You know, Rupert, without me, you never would have known that there is gold down there. I think I deserve a share in the gold."

Rupert started to bounce up and down in the water, causing tidal waves. "Yes, oh, yes! You and me, Edward! A team! We'll become rich! Maybe you can take me back to your world so that I can buy things. Like a hat. I've always wanted a hat."

"You'll be able to have hundreds of hats," Edward said, and he began to think of all the wonderful things he would buy with his money: walkie-talkies, a mini-bike, and a pocket calculator to begin with.

"What shall we do first?" Rupert asked, still bouncing a bit in the water.

"You have to dive to the bottom and scoop up the gold in your mouth. You can drop it over here," he said, pointing to a cleared spot beside the river. Rupert immediately disappeared under the water, and in a minute he was back, emptying a mouthful of mud next to Edward.

"Is that gold?" the serpent asked anxiously.

"It's only wet dirt. You must have been in the wrong spot. Try again."

When Rupert resurfaced, he again brought up a mouthful of mud. Edward frowned. "Can't you do anything? I know it's down there. I saw it when the sun shone on it!"

Rupert hung his head. "I'm sorry. It's so very dark down there. I can't see a thing. Let me try again."

Back in the cave of the winds, the picture in the little pool of water went out of focus.

"I'm so relieved that Edward is safe," Aunt Margaret Matilda said, facing the throne.

"He is safe," echoed the Valley Wind, "but the sooner that boy is home, the better for all of us!"

Holly wasn't quite sure what the wind meant, and there was no way of seeing the wind's expression.

"What should be done about the giant war?" Aunt Margaret Matilda asked.

"Now that you have promised to sit on the Windran throne, be assured that everything will resolve itself," the Mountain Wind said, its powerful voice rustling Holly's hair.

"It will rely on the girl, Holly," the Valley Wind added.

"Me?" Holly asked. "Me?"

"Enough," the Mountain Wind boomed, making Holly jump. "It is time that you joined the others. The giants are preparing their attack. We will help you to return to the elf camp."

With a giggle, the River Wind lifted Holly and Aunt Margaret Matilda up towards the ceiling of the cavern. In the center was a hole that led up into the open sky. They were blown through it, and, once outside, the wind began to fly them over the Windsom Mountains. They saw far below them the two goats that had carried them up the steep trail. "Naaa," the beasts cried when they saw their two passengers flying overhead. Holly waved to them.

"This is the best way to travel! I wish I had a wind to blow me to school every day."

The trees of the forest looked like tiny matchsticks. As they went on, they began a gradual descent, and before they knew it, the elf campsite lay before them. They were let down carefully in the middle of the clearing. The search parties had returned, and the whole camp was stirring with excitement.

"Oh, Your Majesty. I've bad news," said Elf One. "My party didn't see a trace of the boy."

"Mine didn't either," said Elf Two.

"Nor mine," said Elf Three.

At that moment, Suka came in for a landing, panting, with huge tears rolling down his yellow beak. "Suka, the crow, reporting to Her Majesty . . ." he said, and a great gush of tears overcame him." I don't know how to say this," he sniffed, "and it's all my fault because I promised to look after him," he took a sobbing gulp of air, "but the boy, Edward, was thrown into the river by giants!"

Everyone gasped.

"There wasn't anything you could have done, Suka," the queen said kindly. "And don't worry. If you had stayed to watch, you would have seen Edward saved by the river serpent, Rupert."

"Hooray!" the elves cheered.

"We are happy that the child is safe," said Elf One, "but this is no time for talking! The giants are headed this way armed with clubs and spears!"

Aunt Margaret Matilda jumped up. "Elves! Listen quickly. There's not a moment to spare. Get all the children together and put them in the meeting tent. Some of the women and men stay and protect them. Holly, you go, too. The rest of you, arm yourselves and follow me into the forest. We will have a better chance if we ambush them from the trees! Hurry! Everyone get busy!"

Giants Against Elves 9

A few of the elf children began to cry, and one tiny boy started screaming. Holly helped to quiet the little ones and to round up the rest into the meeting tent. All the while, she couldn't stop thinking about what the wind had said: "It will rely on the girl, Holly." How could she help if she was stuck here with the other children? Aunt Margaret Matilda was responsible for her, and that was why she ordered her into the tent. If she disobeyed her aunt and something happened to her, it wouldn't be her aunt's fault. Holly decided to join the fighting in the forest. Wanting to avoid an argument with the elves guarding the opening of the tent, she sneaked out through the back.

The camp was empty. Holly ran to the supply tent. It had been ravaged by the elves in the scurry for weapons, and it looked cleaned out. Holly poked around anyway, hoping to find some sort of sword. Just as she was about to give up the search, a gleam from the floor caught her eye. Sheathed in a jeweled scabbard was a narrow sword! Holly dragged it out into the light and discovered writing on the outside:

On Tiebor the 1ˢᵗ in the Year
of the Winds 4078, this Rapier was presented
to Prince Charles Randolf, Husband of
Windran Queen Elisandra, the Fair.

"This is my grandfather's sword! Maybe it will bring me good luck," Holly exclaimed. "Or, better yet, maybe it's magic!"

When she pulled the rapier from the scabbard, she realized why it had been left behind by the elves. It was very heavy—almost too heavy even for Holly to lift. It had been made for a human man, and Holly was just a little girl.

At last she raised the sword into the air. Its weight caused her to stumble backwards a few steps, and before she could stop herself, she had fallen into one of the wooden bowls used for the celebration dinner. To make matters worse, it wasn't the bowl used for the green salad. It was the still-filled blueberry wine bowl! Holding onto the rapier, Holly sank completely into the purple-blue liquid. When she emerged, she was dyed purple-blue.

Just then, she heard the warning: "The giants are attacking the camp!"

That was bad. Aunt Margaret Matilda had said that they had a better chance in the forest. A group of giants descended on the camp all at once. With their clubs and spears, they wrecked the small tents, and began breaking up everything in sight. The elves were close behind. Too small really to fight the giants, they concentrated on sneaking up behind the huge men and then spearing their feet.

"Good work!" Elf One called to an elf who had just speared the big toe of a giant holding a club. The elf turned around to acknowledge the head elf, and as he bowed, the giant clubbed him over the head and dropped him into a burlap sack containing several other elves. The giants were quickly gathering up all the elves in bags that they intended to drop into the river! Three-quarters of the elves had been caught already, and the others were tired or wounded. None of the giants had been eliminated. A few of them had sore feet, but other than that, they were still strong and fighting.

Holly could see that the elves didn't have a chance. If anything could be done, it would have to be done by her. With a tremendous effort, she leaped from the blueberry wine bowl and attempted to wave the rapier before her.

"En garde!" she shouted, not knowing what it meant, but only that that is what one says when fighting with swords.

Surprised, the giants spun about to see who had shouted the strange words. The blond-haired giant who had thrown Edward into the river was nearest her, and, an evil gleam in his cross-eyes, he began to walk menacingly towards Holly.

With a flash of footwork, Holly tried to ready herself for the oncoming attack, but she could only hold the heavy sword aloft for a few seconds before it sank, useless, to the ground. The blond giant grasped Holly easily around the waist and raised her above his head with low gurgles of giant laughter.

Seeing her niece in a perilous predicament, Aunt Margaret Matilda let out a royal scream. The few fighting elves left what they were doing and rushed to her side. The blond giant, being just clever enough to realize the fuss he had created by grabbing the puny purple child, thought that he might stop the fighting and spare himself some sore toes by using her to his advantage.

"ALL RIGHT," he shouted. "I want the rest of you

elves to give up, or I will crush the life from this girl." He set Holly down under his large, dirty foot.

The elves trembled and looked to their leader for an answer.

"If we give up, you will simply tie us up and throw us into the river," Aunt Margaret Matilda said, trying to give herself a moment to think of a plan.

"That's true," the giant assented. "But if you don't give up, I am going to murder this child right now!"

"Don't listen to him," Holly called out, tears gathering in her eyes. "At least you have a chance if you keep fighting." Was this what the winds had meant by, 'It will rely on the girl, Holly'? Was she to be sacrificed in order that the elves could continue to live in the Windran valley?

"It doesn't matter if you kill the girl," a nasal voice said calmly from the trees. "Haven't you noticed anything strange about her?"

"Who said that?" the giant asked dumbly. Then he took a long look at the girl beneath his foot. "Heh! She's purple!"

"That's right," the nasal voice continued. "And do you know why?"

"No," he answered, scanning the trees for a glimpse of the speaker.

"Because she is going to die—and she is highly contagious."

"What does 'contagious' mean?"

"It means that she has the witch's plague, and that the whole valley is contaminated with it. You're all going to start turning a nice light violet, swelling until you're twice your size. Then the pain will begin! And there's no cure!"

The others backed away several steps, eyeing the blond giant and Holly nervously. Was it true? Was she really contagious?

The poor cross-eyed giant stretched out his hands and gasped. They were a light violet from having touched the blueberry-stained Holly. That was enough to convince him. With a scream, he turned around and ran towards the mountains. Seeing the rest of the giants hesitating, Holly scrambled to her feet and took a few paces in their direction.

"Oh, no! You're not getting near me!" said one, and he took off after the blond-haired giant.

"Let's get out of here," said another.

Soon all the giants could be seen galloping back to the mountains. They were in such a hurry that they forgot about their burlap sacks. Holly ran from one to another, untying and freeing the elves. Aunt Margaret Matilda ran up and gave Holly a kiss and a hug, and all the elves began to bow to her.

"Oh, no," Holly laughed. "Please don't do that."

Aunt Margaret Matilda shook her head. "You can't do a thing about it. Elves are born bowing!"

"I didn't do a thing!" Holly protested. "Clumsy me just fell into the wine bowl. The real hero is whoever thought of the witch's plague. That was genius."

"'Twas nothing. All in the line of duty," the crow's voice came from the trees. "Suka's on the job!"

When everyone settled down, they began the task of dismantling the camp. It was now safe for them to return to the elfin village.

"Dear Windrans, it is getting late, and I must be off with my niece and nephew. I will return, though, to rule the Windran valley," Aunt Margaret Matilda said. Then she helped Holly wash the blueberry stain from her face and hands. The elves happily waved good-by, and the two set off for the river to find Edward.

They had not gone far when someone called, "Wait! Wait for me!" It was Suka. The elves had sent him to accompany the queen and Holly to the river. "And they also wanted me to tell you that the winds said that you have the magical power to open any doors you want."

"We'll need a door back to my bedroom," Holly said. "How much time do you think we have before Mom and Dad will be home?"

"Not very much, I'm afraid. It will be close."

The first thing they saw when they reached the river's edge was a towering pile of mud. Rupert was resting his head on the bank while Edward paced back and forth. "It has to be there. I saw it, I know I did."

"Are you ready to go home?" Aunt Margaret Matilda asked sweetly.

"I can't go now. Rupert and I are gold mining."

"So then you admit that this is no dream?" Holly teased.

Edward bit his lip and grimaced at his sister. "What happened to your clothes? You're a purple mess!"

"I hate to be the one to tell you," Holly went on, "but there is no gold. So you see, the giants were really fighting for nothing."

"No gold?" There was a sad expression on Rupert's face.

"I saw it," Edward insisted.

"And when you went down to the bottom, what did you find?" Holly asked.

"Just Rupert."

"Exactly."

"Huh?" said the serpent.

Edward smacked his hand to his forehead. "It was only the reflection of Rupert's golden scales! Aauugh!"

All Rupert said was, "No hat . . ."

"There's our door. It's time to go, children."

Holly and Edward followed Aunt Margaret Matilda's gaze. A familiar door had appeared on the river bank.

"Good-by, Suka. You are the smartest crow I ever met," Holly said, and she placed a kiss atop the bird's feathery head.

Rupert was crying gigantic tears. "Oh, Edward, do you have to leave? And Margaret Matilda, you've just come back. Are you going, too?"

"I'll be back," she winked, and Rupert stopped his blubbering.

"Looks like we have to break up the team, Rupert. Sorry I made you work for nothing," apologized Edward.

Rupert smiled. "That's all right. It's the most fun I've had in years."

"Let's go." The wind picked up around them and the door ahead opened. They could see the inside of Holly's bedroom with the embroidered pictures on either side of the closet door. With one powerful puff of wind, they sailed through the doorway. There was a slam behind them and then silence.

Home Again | 10

"HELLO! Anyone home?" came a voice from downstairs.

"It's Mom and Dad!"

The three sat nervously on Holly's bed while the vacationers climbed the stairs. "Are we ever glad to be home," Mr. Randolf said as he entered the room. "Did you miss us?"

"We were kind of busy," Edward shrugged.

"Doing *what*?" asked Mrs. Randolf in a shocked voice. "Holly, what have you gotten all over your clothes?" Holly surveyed her purple-stained outfit. "And Edward! Where did all that mud come from?" He looked down to where his boots had carried dirt all over the carpet.

Aunt Margaret Matilda smiled. "They may be a little dirty, but they're safe and sound."

"I never worried a minute," said Mr. Randolf. "Not with my sister watching them."

Mrs. Randolf looked doubtful. "You two had better go and get washed up," she said to Holly and Edward. "Did they behave for you, Margaret Matilda?"

"Good as gold," she said lightly. "Now, if you will excuse me, I would like to pack my things."

"Leaving already?" protested Mr. Randolf. "We've hardly had time to talk."

"I have pressing business elsewhere."

Holly and Edward shared a smile.

"I thought I told you two to wash up," reprimanded Mrs. Randolf. "Get going."

By the time Holly and Edward had bathed and changed their clothes, Aunt Margaret Matilda was standing by the door with her coat on and her suitcase in hand. Holly wrapped her arms about her aunt.

"You will come back, won't you?"

"I promise," the pixy-faced lady nodded.

Edward came close to his aunt holding something crushed in his hand. It was his baseball cap. "Please give this to Rupert," he whispered.

Aunt Margaret Matilda pushed the hat into her

pocket and smiled. "Time for me to go. I love you all. Good-by!" the tiny woman said, and she started off down the steps. Holly and Edward lingered on the stoop, watching Aunt Margaret Matilda walk away.

"Did it really happen?" Holly asked. "We have nothing to prove that it wasn't just an exciting dream."

In the distance, they saw Aunt Margaret Matilda approach a door that was standing all by itself in the middle of the street. She opened it, went through, and disappeared!

The children stood a minute without saying a word.

"It's probable that we will never get back to Windra," Holly sighed.

Her brother winked at her. "But it's always possible that we shall!"

Holly closed the front door and, together, they went to play.